LEAP for LITERACY

LIBRARY
WITH STAN TUCKER

Dear Fellow Story Explorers,

Thank you for picking up this extraordinary book! You are holding a unique text, the culmination of many helping hands and one remarkable young author. A young author who participated in an exciting and interactive writing program called Share Your Story!

Share Your Story is a nationally acclaimed writing program which mentors aspiring authors through an eight-step writing process. Opportunities to interact virtually with published authors are provided so that participants gain insight and feedback about their new craft! This program addresses barriers that may prevent students from participating in meaningful literacy experiences.

Leap for Literacy offers several initiatives, including Read-N-Roll, which uses kindness as the currency for students to build their personal collection of books, the Read-It-Forward-athon which is a fundraiser fueled by minutes read and acts of kindnes, and the Leap For Literacy Publishing Program. This program allows students from the Share Your Story Program the opportunity to submit their books for consideration to be published and professionally illustrated!

You are holding a true labor of love! Please share this powerful book with another Story Explorer and support our mission to create meaningful literacy opportunities for students in our community and across our country.

Yours in Learning,

Stanley T Tucker

Stanley T. Tucker
Founder, Leap for Literacy
Host of The Very Airy Library

LEAP *for* LITERACY

www.leapforliteracy.org

ZENOVIA

Written by Leta De Giorgi

Illustrations by Diana Resendiz

This Book Belongs to:

_____

_____

This book is dedicated to everyone who supported me in my writing journey, you know who you are.

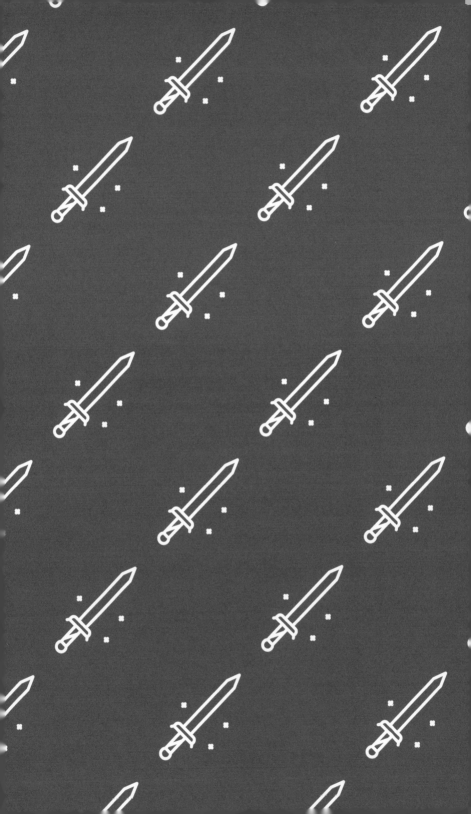

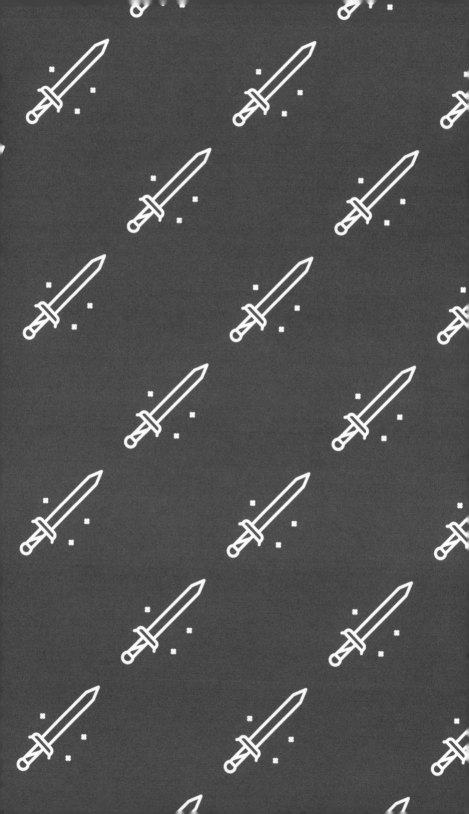

Chapter One
Plot twist

I rushed through the cold alleyway as gentle snowflakes drifted through the air. Once I was a safe distance from the market, I slowed my pace. Suddenly, I felt the ground sweep up from beneath my feet. I heard a loud crack as I hit the concrete. Head spinning and blood trickling from my mouth, I gasped in pain. My pockets bulged with the apples and sausages I had swiped from the market, and two angry firbolgs hovered above me, one with a pan and the other with a long wooden pole, both with angry expressions. They were the firbolgs from the market, and let's just say they don't like giving away free stuff.

"We warned you not to steal our food," said the one holding the pole in a gruff voice, his beady green eyes fixed on mine.

He was tall with pointed ears and a massive body. His comrade, slightly smaller but still three times my size, nodded in agreement. In the dim darkness of the alleyway, I could still make out the mark under each of their eyes. Verum.

They had caught me off guard; I'm usually a good fighter, but I was already impaired by the blow to my head. Ignoring the comment, I took a shaky breath and got to my feet. I swung my fist at the smaller one, the impact causing him to stumble back. Instantly, I swung my head back, ready to throw a punch at the other. It was too late, the firbolgs's wooden pole came swinging through the air into my ribcage, sending me into a nearby pile of cardboard boxes. I wanted to get up, but I couldn't.

When I was born, I was a perfect child, but no matter what I did, they would always expect me to fail. It didn't matter how good I was now; I would always end up in Enchendale, the largest and the only prison in the kingdom. Zenovia, the kingdom I live in, is a magical place with breathtaking sights and terrifying monsters. From Elves to Dragons, there are many unique creatures. There are busy cities and ancient rural lands.

Everyone in Zenovia is born with a mark under their eye: ග for Verum or ᑫ for Malus. If you are Verum, you're safe. If you're Malus, you're destined to grow to be a criminal and eventually end up with every other Malus in Echendale. Only the fates could decide what mark someone would receive, and they decide it long before birth, determining how a life will play out before it even begins. That was just how it went; it was just up to fate. For hundreds of years, everyone was either Verum or Malus, no plot twists, no exceptions, until the year 438 when I was born. I was the plot twist; I was the first one that didn't have a ග or ᑫ mark. I had both.

Chapter Two
I'm leaving

I couldn't get caught for this. They would throw me in that stupid jail forever!

The rough brick wall scraped my hand as I grasped it for balance. Reaching back, I pulled my dagger, the family heirloom my grandma gave me, out of its casing. Grandma was the only person who believed I wasn't Malus, that I had some other purpose in life than to be sent to Enchendale. Staggering, I pushed off the wall to face the firbolgs.

They inched closer to me, their attack impending, and a low growl sounded from behind me. A dark shadow crept up the wall. Whipping my head around, I searched to see what was making the sound and traced it to a cardboard box. Behind the box, and out of the sight of the firbolgs, was a scruffy-looking dog.

The dog had greasy black fur that was brown from the dirt covering it. It looked like it hadn't eaten in weeks.

The firbolgs stiffened in fear, and I, trying my best to look scared, backed away from the box. Their eyes darted from me to the box, and then, just like that, they were out of there, stumbling over one another to get away from the sound.

Once they were out of earshot, I burst into laughter. The shadow stopped growing, and the dog looked at me curiously.

"Did you see their faces?" I asked the dog, half-jokingly, "Holy fates, that was hilarious."

The dog's tail wagged happily. It walked up to me and licked my hand. I stroked its filthy fur and gazed into its sea-blue eyes. Then, I felt something I hadn't felt in a long time. Love. There was something special about this dog. "Hey bud, I have a journey I need to go on," the dog looked back at me, "Wanna come along?"

Walking in the direction of my house, I beckoned the dog to follow. He trotted happily by my side as I made my way through the town, getting the usual dirty looks from passersby. Only when we reached the large vine-ridden stone house with the tattered shingles did we stop, and I stepped inside.

The dog followed me up the stairs to the bathroom, where I put him inside the shower. "You need a little bit of a rinse-off before I go anywhere with you," I said, eyeing his filthy state. I turned the knob to turn the water on and I rinsed him off. Once I had turned the water off and he was looking better, we went into my room and I began to pack. I gathered only what I would need for my journey; clothes, The Book of Dragons, travel supplies, and then, after a thought, I grabbed my silver necklace and hung it around my neck. It had been a gift from my mom, one of the only ones she'd given me.

I glanced over at my nightstand to a small glass container holding a purple paste. I knew that would come in handy. Pocketing the container, I looked around to see if there was anything I had forgotten. Satisfied with my preparation and planning, I grabbed a pen off my desk and started to write.

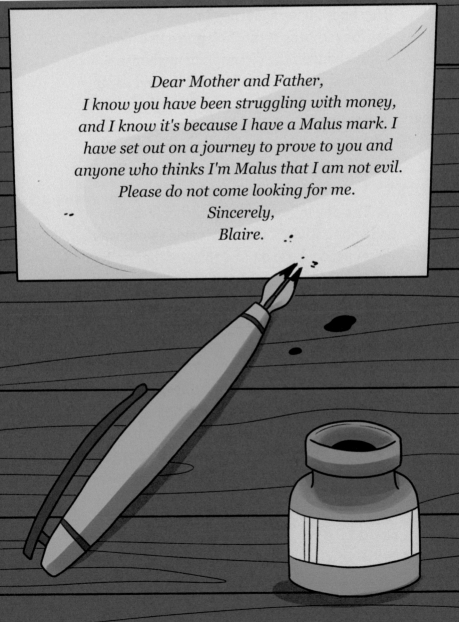

Dear Mother and Father,
I know you have been struggling with money, and I know it's because I have a Malus mark. I have set out on a journey to prove to you and anyone who thinks I'm Malus that I am not evil. Please do not come looking for me.
Sincerely,
Blaire.

Outside, the cool air was refreshing. With a deep breath, I went over my plan: to travel to the town of Danshana and defeat Cromic. Cromic, the lava dragon, had been in an eternal slumber but mysteriously awakened and was terrorizing the people of Danshana. If I could put Cromic back into his eternal slumber, then I could come home and be pronounced a hero. I could finally prove I wasn't Malus. My family and I could move to a wealthier town and live out our lives with loads of money, and maybe people would stop hating me so much. After my parents first met, they opened a bakery together. It started small, but soon, they were producing almost all of the baked goods in town. When I was born, things began to change. Because of my Malus mark, people were afraid to buy from my parents, and they eventually had to shut down. Now, we live in poverty, desperate enough that I began to, on occasion, steal food from the town's market, which had worked until today.

The familiar scents of the horses greeted me as I walked over to the stables.

Windy, the last remaining horse whom I had begged my parents not to sell, awaited me. I saddled Windy up and paused, would the dog be able to keep up with Windy? The dog was looking at me expectantly as if to say, "Let's go already!"

I gently kicked my heels against the side of the horse, and the dog trotted alongside us as if we'd been traveling partners all of our lives. I watched as the town I had grown to love got smaller and smaller until it was out of sight.

Chapter Three
Banshee

As the sun made its way down the horizon, we found ourselves a ways away from our destination and needing to seek shelter for the night. We continued trotting along until I spotted a figure in the distance - it could be a traveler who could point us in the direction of a tavern nearby!
We approached them, and I dismounted Windy, reined her to a nearby tree, and stepped forward. That's when I began to feel that something was off. The figure, robed in a worn, dark cloak that covered its face, seemed to be hovering above the ground.

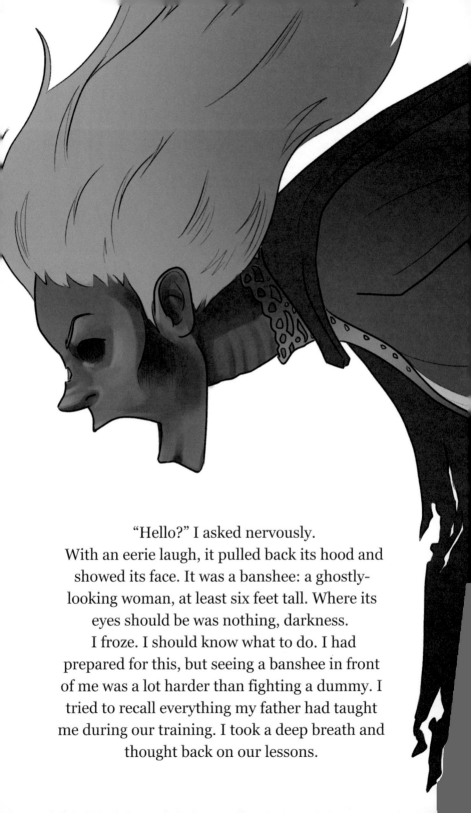

"Hello?" I asked nervously.
With an eerie laugh, it pulled back its hood and
showed its face. It was a banshee: a ghostly-
looking woman, at least six feet tall. Where its
eyes should be was nothing, darkness.
I froze. I should know what to do. I had
prepared for this, but seeing a banshee in front
of me was a lot harder than fighting a dummy. I
tried to recall everything my father had taught
me during our training. I took a deep breath and
thought back on our lessons.

One cold evening, we sat by the fire. We had just finished our lesson on controlling my fire abilities when my father pulled out The Book of Monsters, the book he read whenever it was time for me to learn how to fight a new monster.

"Banshees are the spirits of evil elves. In life, the elves used their beauty to manipulate. Upon their death, they were turned to banshees as punishment," his voice was deep but soothing, "To kill a banshee, you need to cut the back of its neck. Now, this doesn't kill them immediately. A banshee can live up to five hours after you cut their neck, but it will slow them enough to let you get away."

He paused and gestured to his neck, showing me the place where the cut would need to be made.

- another thing I'd need to practice when training-

"That's why they are so dangerous."

I looked up at his face; it was stern but loving. His eyes twinkled in the firelight. I could feel the heat from the flames emanating on my skin.

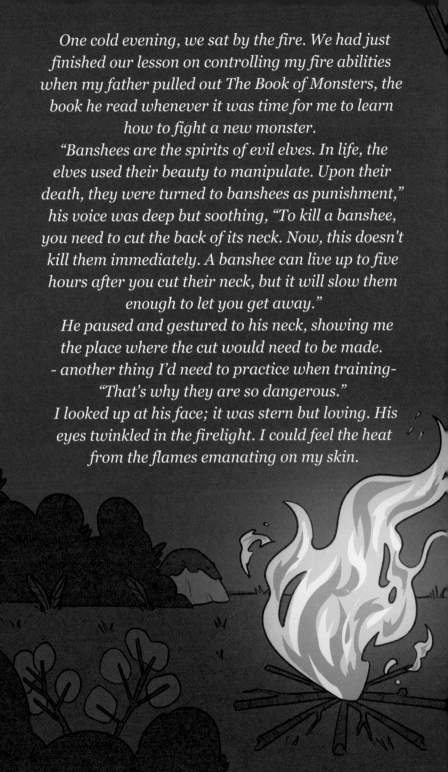

The memory faded away, and I was back, face to face with my childhood nightmare: a banshee.

The dog let out a low growl, inching closer to the Banshee. I stepped in front of the dog, shielding him from the Banshee, and felt for the dagger behind my back.

"L-look," I said shakily, trying my best to conceal my fear, "If-if you let us pa-ass, then we won't cause you any trouble."

"You? Cause me trouble? You are in my territory now; you don't stand a chance against me."

Its voice, deep and scratchy, ran a chill down my spine.

The Banshee lunged at me. Adrenaline kicked in, and my training became instinctive. I dodged to the side, trying to slash at its back, but it had already circled toward me. Its cloak swayed aside, revealing a tattered dress underneath and a leather belt sheathing at least a dozen daggers.

My heart pounded as I took up my stance in front of the Banshee. The dog, unable to assist in the fight, barked wildly. The banshee smirked, grabbing a dagger with each hand. She threw her hand back and flung the daggers at me. I ducked just in time, the daggers whizzing over my head and into a nearby tree, making a thunking sound as they stuck firmly into the bark. I rose, but the banshee was already throwing the second round of knives, one just missing my foot and the other narrowly missing my face, but not without leaving a mark. I scrambled toward Windy as another dagger struck the ground beside me.

I crouched behind a nearby tree to regain my breath, and a second later, I was dashing at the Banshee, dagger in hand, ready to attack. The Banshee, startled by my sudden reappearance, was weaponless. Before she could grab another dagger from her belt, I pounced on her and pinned her to the ground. Her skin burned against mine.

"Their skin is like acid; it will burn you easily if you are not careful."

I had to withstand the pain if I wanted to kill the banshee. I pressed my dagger against the back of her neck... and I hesitated. How could I kill someone? But I trained for this, and it was the banshee or me.

Quickly, I stabbed my dagger into the back of her throat. The banshee let out a shriek and flailed on the ground.

Quickly, I got to my feet and mounted my Windy. We took off towards a faint light in the distance. I glanced back to get one more look at the Banshee shriveling pain and rage. The dog was following beside me, seeming very happy to have made it out alive and in one piece.

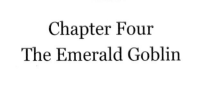

Chapter Four
The Emerald Goblin

We arrived at the Emerald Goblin, an old, rundown tavern in the middle of nowhere. When I asked how close we were to Danshana, the tavern owner told us we were two hours away from Syra Bay and at least another day's trip from Danshana. He was a grae, a short creature with dull green skin, and was clearly intoxicated. He had floppy ears and a verum mark on his left cheek.

"You got a place we can stay the night?" I asked the wobbly tavern owner.

"Yep, room…" He paused as if this were a tough question, "Three," he replied with a tired, drunken look on his face.

Luckily, he was too out of it to notice I had both Verum and Malus marks. I was handing him six gold pieces in exchange for a card stamped with red ink when he noticed my reddened hand.

"Ooh, did'a fight a banshee?" He asked, gesturing to my hand.

"Yeah, nasty thing," I responded casually.

"Here," he reached under the counter and rummaged around for a bit, "Ah ha!"

He pulled out a jar with hundreds of dead spiders in it;
I caught myself trying not to gag, I hate spiders. He
looked at me, then at the jar.

"Oops, wrong jar."

He rummaged around a bit more until he came up with
a jar of bluish-green gel. Grinning, he handed it to me.
"Put it on, it's a cooling gel, it'll help with the... The
thingy, you know, the banshee. That thing has been
scaring off customers for months."

I stood there, perplexed. Why would he give this to me?
I made my way to room three and set my bag next to
the nightstand. I hesitated, then grabbed the jar that the
tavern owner had given me and spun the lid off. Trying
to ignore my aversion to the gooey texture, I dipped in
my pointer finger, and the heat instantly subsided. With
a sigh of relief, I quickly put some on the rest of my
hand.

After quickly washing up and storing my belongings, I grabbed some carrots and went to the stable to tend to Windy. There was only one other horse; there must not be many visitors.

"Hey bud," I said as I stroked the horse, "Why did the tavern owner give me that gel?"

Thankfully, the horse didn't respond. Content that Windy was washed and watered, I walked to the small weapons shop near the tavern and meandered through the aisles. I had left my dagger in the banshee's throat, and there was no way I was going to continue traveling weaponless. Most of my training had been with daggers, so I was looking for something similar when I heard, "I heard baselards are good."

Turning to the voice, I was faced by a siren. His body was covered in iridescent blue and silver scales shimmering in the light of the shop, and his tail slowly swayed back and forth, making a soft scraping sound as it brushed the wooden floor.

"Uhh... Hi, do you know much about weapons?" I asked awkwardly.

"Yeah, my dad is a blacksmith, so I know a thing or two about them, are you having trouble finding something? I heard you talking to yourself."

"I was talking to myself?" I could feel my cheeks turning red.

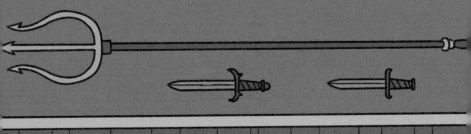

"Yeah, you were," he said smiling, "Anyways, baselards aren't that popular of a choice but are really handy. They are built to be small and swift, just like a dagger. They are shorter than a short sword but longer than a dagger. It would probably be perfect for you."

He paused and looked at me as if waiting for an answer.

"Uh, yeah, sure, do you have one?" I asked.

"No, but I saw one over here. Follow me," He said, gesturing for me to follow.

He headed toward a corner near the back of the store, stopping in front of a small pedestal encased by glass. Inside lay a shiny silver baselard, exactly how he described it. My hands went to lift the glass case, but then I spotted the price tag. My heart sank, and I withdrew my hands from the glass.

"Two hundred gold pieces," I said grimly.
"Yeah, not too bad for one in this condition," he
paused, studying my face,
"You can't afford it, can you," he asked.
"No," I responded sheepishly.
"How much do you have?"
"Enough to buy myself food and a place to sleep, I
wasn't expecting to have to buy a weapon," I
admitted.
"Oh, what do you need a weapon for anyway?"
"Well, I need money for my family, so I'm on a
journey to end Cromic's wrath."
He looked surprised.
"Well, I was also on a quest, but someone beat me to
it. I am on my way to Syra Bay right now...Do you
mind if I join you on your quest?"
I considered, and before I could change my mind,
said, "Yes! I mean, no, I don't mind... But haven't you
noticed? I have two marks."
"Yeah, I saw, but just because one of them is a Malus
mark doesn't make you Malus."
He smiled, and I smiled back.
"You can call me Blaire, and you are?"
"Falen, nice to meet you, Blaire. Now, are you still
interested in that baselard?"
"Yes, can you afford it?"
"Yeah, I'll meet you tomorrow in the stable, okay?"

On the walk back to the room, I was unsure if I had
made the right choice. I had made a deal with a
complete stranger. He did help me find a weapon,
and he is paying for it, and he is Verum, so I guess he
can't betray me. Sighing, I went into my room.
The dog, who had become my shadow, looked up at
me with sparkling eyes. Sitting on the floor and
petting his head, I mused, "You should have a name.
What about... Smokey. No, that just sounds weird."
I stared at the dog, trying to think.
"Whatcha looking at buddy?" I asked him, following
the dog's eyes to a painting of a forest with a small
badger in the center, "Well, that's an interesting art
choice."
I looked back at the dog, his black face was streaked
with white, just like the badger in the painting.
"What about Badger?"

He wagged its tail and rubbed his nose into my hand.
"Badger it is!"
Badger came closer, licking my face.
"Eeww Badger!"
My cheek burned, only for a second, and then it stopped.
"Wait, what?"
I gingerly touched my cheek. It was smooth; the small cut from where the banshee's dagger nicked my face was gone. Standing up, I looked in the mirror; my purple skin was smooth, as if the cut was never there.
"Whoa, was that you, Badger?"
The dog wagged its tail, and I sat back down next to him.
"I've never heard of a dog that can heal. You are special, aren't you, Badger?"
Stroking his fur affectionately, I thought back to our first encounter. Back in the alleyway, I'd been bleeding and hurt after those firbolgs attacked. But then, Badger licked me after. I had been too relieved to notice, but there was no way I would have been able to fight the banshee if Badger hadn't healed me. A special dog, indeed.

The next day, I woke bright and early. As planned, Falen met me at the stable, baselard in hand. "Here you go," he said, handing me the weapon. "Thanks," I replied, sliding the weapon into its sheath at my back. The loss of my dagger saddened me, but this was definitely an upgrade. "You ready?" I asked Falen. "As ready as I'll ever be." With a flick of our reigns, we were off.

Chapter Five
Syra Bay

After what felt like ages of travel and definitely more than the two hours that the tavern owner had suggested, we made it to Syra Bay. We stabled our horses, and with my hood up and head down, I tried to blend in as much as possible.

"I know a place where we can stop for lunch, then we can continue traveling. I'm not sure if we'll make it to Danshana tonight; we might need to stay in a town nearby," said Falen in a hushed voice.

"Why are we whispering?" I asked, mimicking his quiet tone.

"I don't know, why are you hiding?" He replied, louder now.

"My mark... Oh, I know," I reached into my pocket and pulled out my container of purple paste.

"What's that?" Falen asked curiously.

"My mom gave it to me, it's to cover up my malus mark," I said, dipping my finger in the goo.

He pursed his lips but didn't say anything. Once I had applied the paste, Falen confirmed he couldn't see my malus mark, and we headed further into town.

"Here we are," said Falen, stopping in front of a small restaurant with brick walls and low-hanging lantern lights.

It looked just like the restaurants in my hometown. The nostalgia hit me like a wave, from the way it looked to the way it smelled to the music that was humming in the background. I thought about my parents and hoped the food I got would last them until I got back.

We walked inside and sat ourselves at a table, a family of elves was seated nearby.

"She is fine, I promise!"

The pleading tone jolted me from my thoughts. I glanced toward the family; a waiter was making a sour expression at the little girl. On the girl's cheek was a malus mark.

"I need to talk to my manager. Don't order anything, and keep her away from other customers," he said bitterly.

"What is his problem?" I whispered to Falen, glancing toward the waiter.

"It's not that uncommon; I'm sure you have experienced it too, right?"

Falen was right; I had experienced similar hardships during my life. Suddenly, I wasn't so fond of this place.

"Yeah, I guess so,"

We sat in silence for a moment until I picked up the newspaper on the table and read aloud, "Sirens Vade and Kaleb Deeren Stop Infamous Gang of Half-Orcs."

"Wait! Really?" exclaimed Falen, snatching the newspaper from my hands.

He scanned the page, and his expression darkened.

"Good for them," He said sarcastically.

"What?" I asked, confused by his sullen tone.

"Nothing, I mean... fine. Those are my brothers," he confessed.

"And this means?" I asked, still very confused.

"You know how I told you I was on a quest? Well, it was to stop that group. I was just over halfway there before someone told me they had already been captured. I didn't know it was them," he said, pointing at the picture of his brothers.

"And you are upset because they beat you to it?"
"Yeah, they are the perfect children, after all."
"Do they do that a lot?"
"Steal my mission or get the headline of the newspaper?"
"Both."
"Well, usually I don't go on missions, and the ones I have been on, my brothers haven't intervened because they were deemed too unimportant for them. But they get the headline a lot. They're the most well-known sirens in the town. I thought if I could stop that gang, I might be seen for once. No one pays attention to me, not anyone besides my dad. He was-"
Falen was cut off by the waiter. We ordered our food and devoured it instantly. Falen didn't bring up his dad or his brothers anymore, and although I was curious, I didn't ask about it. Instead, I told Falen about how Badger had healed me the night before.
"What? There's no way! How is that even possible?"
"When you showed me the baselard, did you notice I had a cut on my cheek?"
"No," he said.

"Well, there was a cut on my face, and when Badger licked me, it disappeared. The same thing happened when I was fighting some firbolgs. They had hit me with this wooden-"

Falen cut me off before I could finish.

"Why were you fighting firbolgs? They usually try to avoid conflict."

"That's none of your business," I snapped at him, then, instantly regretting my harsh tone, "Look, the important thing is that I was pretty beaten up, but after Badger licked me, I was okay again. I didn't even realize it until he healed me the second time."

"Weird, I've never heard of that,"

We had paid for lunch and continued through Syra Bay to a shop Falen showed me to get some kibble for Badger.

"Why couldn't I just order him a steak?"

"Because dog food is better for him, trust me,"
He said, patting Badger's head as we walked.
We walked into the pet store, and Falen
showed me around, enthusiastically picking
out the different things we'd need for Badger.
"Is all this stuff really necessary? He has been
living on the streets for who knows how long,
let's just get a couple of canned meals and
head to Danshana."
"Fine. If you lose your magic dog because he
doesn't have a collar, that's your fault."
We paid and left, heading back over to the
local horse stables. I gave Badger a can of dog
food; it smelled horrendous.
"Eww, what's in this stuff?" I asked, eyeing
the gooey contents of the can.
"I don't know, and I don't want to know," said
Falen, just as disgusted.
I glanced at the town's clock tower and
realized it was already after two.
"We should get going," I said, swinging my leg
over Windy.
Falen glanced back into the town, then got on
his horse.

Chapter Six
Volcano

We rode through the mountains, careful to follow the path on my map. Falen had warned that the mountains were easy to get lost in. We meandered through the hills, chatting about Badger, weapons, and the breathtaking views of the mountains. The closer we got to our destination, the hotter it got, it was noticeably warmer than the cool winds of Syra Bay. We were anxious; we hadn't wanted to talk about how we were on our way to fight one of the most powerful beings in the land. But no matter how anxious we were, if we didn't have a plan, we wouldn't have a chance at beating Cromic.

"We need to come up with a plan." I finally blurted out.

"You're saying you don't have one?" Falen exclaimed.

"I do, but you need to help, too, I don't know much about sirens, what can you do?" I asked

"I have a crossbow that I can use. It's my favorite weapon; not too fragile and precise like an elf's bow, but it's long-distance, and it deals a good amount of damage," he said proudly.

"Great, anything else?"

He seemed taken aback by my lack of interest in the weapon.

"Um, I have enhanced siren senses. I can manipulate water in small amounts... although there is no water at a volcano." He said, frowning.

"OK, so what's your plan? You said you had one, so let's hear it," said Falen.

"Well, first things first, we need to find this guy called Azar, a Dragonborn, he is supposedly the son of a keeper, you know what a keeper is, right?"

"I somewhat know about them, but I could use a refresher."

"Keepers are a special class of people. They all still have marks, although they are probably all verum, and they are still from different races, but they are specially chosen and trained to be a keeper. They undergo intense training, then are brought to the underground lake, Lake Opal, where they perform a ritual. Only the keepers know where Lake Opal is and what happens during the ritual.

Unfortunately, over the years, the keepers seemed to die out, and the ancient ritual was lost. But some remain, they say they are trying to bring keepers back, but so far, they have been unsuccessful. Azar, the only recorded keeper in Dashana, inherited his mother's powers - it's extremely rare but has been known to happen from time to time. He'll be trying to stop Cromic as well, and we can't put Cromic back into his eternal slumber without him." I explained.

Falen, after listening intently, considered, "What do we do from there?"

"Azar needs to work a spell on Cromic, in the meantime, he'll need us to create a distraction. Make sense?"

"Pretty much, but what guarantees that we'll find Azar?"

"There is no guarantee," I confessed.

"Exhilarating," said Falen sarcastically.

Nerves overcame me. I had been planning this for so long, but what if it didn't work? My anxiety rose with each step toward our destination.

"You ok?" asked a voice, it seemed so distant.

"W-what?" I asked the voice.

My head was spinning, and I felt lightheaded. I wobbled, unsteady on Windy's back, then darkness.

Smack, a sharp pain struck my face. What happened? We still trotted along the same path. I looked over at Falen, who was staring at me apprehensively.

"What- what just happened?" I asked him, my head still spinning.

"You weren't responding to me, then you just collapsed on your horse. You're lucky you didn't fall off," explained Falen.

"Did you hit me?"

"Yeah, to get you to wake up, and it worked," said Falen.

"It's getting hot," I remarked drowsily.

"We are getting closer to the volcano," he said. I wiped away the sweat beading on my forehead. Reaching into my saddle bag for water, my hand brushed a jar. I pulled it out; it was the ointment from the tavern owner.

"Didn't he say this was cooling gel?"

"What?" asked Falen, confused.

"I was talking to myself. I got this cooling gel from the tavern owner at the Emerald Goblin, he said it would help with a burn on my hand, I think it could help with the heat, too."

Dipping my two fingers into the thick gel instantly cooled my skin down. Even in the hot temperature, the gel remained icy cold. I smeared some on my face and neck, then rubbed more on my arms and legs. The relief was instant, and my head was once again clear.

"Want some?" I asked, holding the jar out to Falen.

"I'm ok, being a siren lets me stay cool, even when I'm in hot environments," he explained.

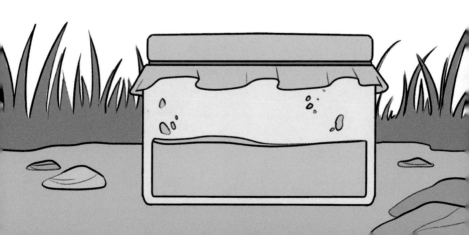

"That's handy," I said, screwing the lid back on, "Do you think I passed out from the heat?" "Probably, you should drink some water and make sure you keep reapplying that gel." Nodding in agreement, I downed half the water in my canteen, and we continued our trek through the mountains. It was oddly peaceful, considering where the road led. The only audible sounds were the rustle of the trees and birds, the tapping of the horse's hooves on the dirt path, and a faint gurgling sound. At first, I thought it was the river in the canyon to our left, but I realized that the sound was coming from the right. Falen must have heard it as well, as we simultaneously turned and froze. In front of us lay an enormous red blob, a blazeorb. As it intently hopped along, I hoped it hadn't noticed us.

"What is that?" Exclaimed Falen.

The blazeorb, a giant molten glob with glowing holes where its mouth and eyes should be, turned to look at us. It opened its mouth and roared, sending little bits of goo flying at us as it advanced.

Hastily, Falen and I grabbed our weapons and dismounted. He held his dagger and glared at the blazeorb. Curiously, it closed its mouth and looked at us. Then, it launched itself at Falen.

Falen slashed with his dagger, piercing right through it. The blazeorb split in two and splattered to the ground, dead. Relief briefly flooded through me before... Wait, they don't die so easily.

Two blobs began forming from the ground, each with glowing eyes and mouths trained on Falen.

"They don't die, they multiply!" I screamed at Falen.

With a horrified glance, he hollered, "Then how do we kill them?"

"Water!" I screamed back at him.

The rushing river was too far, but my canteen was still half-full and could buy the time I needed. In a dash, I turned to Windy and grabbed at my sack, fumbling with the clip in my desperation to get to the canteen.

"A blazeorb is hundreds of degrees, one touch can cause a third-degree burn," my father had told me - He didn't say much more about them, there wasn't much to say; they were giant jelly-like blobs that were scorching hot.

Finally, I got the bag to open and grabbed the canteen.

"Falen! Use this to hold them off while I get more water from the river!" I yelled, running back towards him as I unscrewed the lid.

"Okay!" He shouted back, sheathing his dagger and grabbing the canteen.

He splashed water out at the blazeorb, causing them to sizzle and shrink back.

The side of the mountain was steep and rocky, one wrong step, and I would go tumbling down. Quickly, I stepped around the rocks, careful not to catch my foot on a loose one. The grunts and gurgling from the Falen's stand-off faded as I reached the river, the roaring sounds of the water drowning out the sound. I took off my hood, grateful for the strong material, filled it with water, and rushed back to Falen, where he now faced four blazeorbs.

"I killed one with the water, but I need more!" Cried Falen. Frantically swinging his dagger to keep them away,

"I got some!" I yelled.

He tossed his dagger to the side and concentrated on moving the water towards himself. The blazeorbs, looking intimidated, cautiously backed away.

Now, in a bubble in front of Falen, the water began shaping into large spikes. With a sizzle, the spikes shot through the globs. Muffled gurgles echoed through the mountains as the blobs melted away, leaving only steam behind.

"Are you ok?" I asked, turning to Falen.
"A little shaken up but fine, you?" He responded,
wiping the sweat off his forehead.
"Yeah," I confirmed.
"That was hard," he said wearily.
"I bet. Do you want to go get some water from the
creek?"
"Sure."
We headed down the slope, this time slowly.
Falen told me about what had happened when I
went to get the water from the river; how he
defeated one of the blazeorbs, but the remaining
one quadrupled as he tried to defend himself with
his dagger.
After enjoying the fresh, cool water and refilling
our canteens, we walked back up the slope to our
horses and continued our journey. I watched the
sun slipping behind the mountain, and soon again,
we were encased under the night's veil of
darkness.

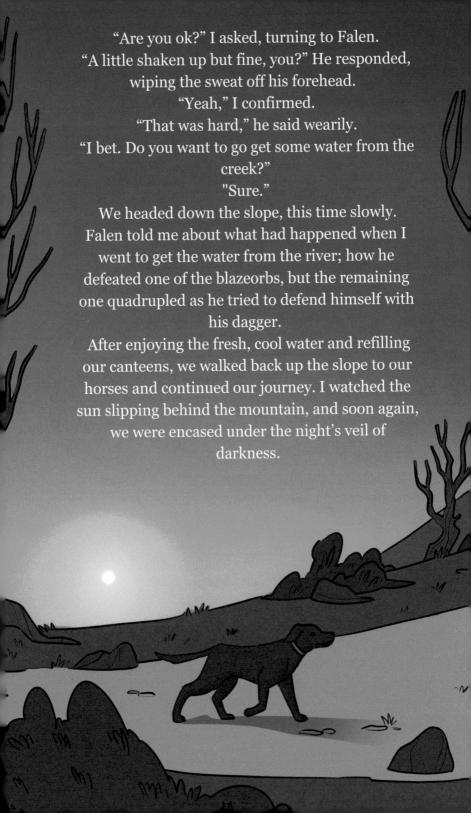

Chapter Seven
The Beginning of the end

Finally, we reached Danshana. The sun had gone down about an hour ago, and we needed to find a place to stay the night.

"I know we've been up all day, but don't you think we should look for Azar?" asked Falen.

"I don't know..." I paused. I was drowsy, but we did need to find Azar, "Alright, but let's try to make it quick, and let's pick up some food on the way."

"Sounds good," agreed Falen.

We wandered through the town; the cobblestone roads were covered in ash, and the houses were small, made with bricks or stones to better withstand the fiery landscape. We stopped by a small shop to pick up some food. We each got a large sandwich, and we ate as we walked, peering into windows and stopping in occasional stores to inquire about Azar.

We entered a small library where a teenage girl, a Fyrian like me, sat behind the counter. She had long curling horns, a long, spiked tail, and a Verum mark on her cheek.

"Oh! Hello, hello, hello," she exclaimed, dropping the book she was reading as she approached us, "How may I help you today? What are you looking for?"

"Has anyone named Azar been here? He's pretty tall, he's a dragonborn..."

"Oh, yes! He was reading this!" She said, handing me a book, All About Dragons. Cromic's crimson red eye looked up at me menacingly from the cover, the other eye no more than a scarred slit. The deep red and amber of his scales glowed in the light of the volcano as he spread his wings above it. I took the book from her hands and flipped to the section about Cromic.

"Cromic is an extremely strong dragon, one of the most powerful in all the land," I read, well, that's comforting, *"Cromic can be defeated one of two ways: 1. You can retrieve the gemstone from the town hall so a keeper can use an arokgranvia spell, which will put Cromic into an eternal slumber and make the volcano dormant, or; 2. By slaying him, however, be warned, this will not make the volcano dormant."*

I handed the book back to the girl.
"Thank you. Do you know where he was going?"
"No, I'm sorry, I don't, but would you like to
check out this book?" She asked.
"Sure," I replied.
We took the book and began looking for a place
to spend the night.

"No, Tamara, we are going to the tavern. We will
deal with it in the morning," Grumbled a
dragonborn walking past us.
It took me a moment to process what I had just
seen; Azar, the key to defeating Cromic, just
walked in front of me. Before I could think, my
legs sprinted towards him. I ran in front of him,
blocking his path.

Azar was tall, at least six feet, with a large, muscular body covered in scales. He had horns on his head and a dragon tail peeking out from behind the greatsword he wore sheathed at his waist. His black eyes fixed on mine, I fumbled with my words, trying to find what to say.

"Uh, hi, you don't know me, but my name is Blaire, I'm from a small village up north called Skrix, I am a good fighter, and I heard about you, and I want to help you defeat Cromic," the information poured out of my mouth as my hands began to sweat and I bit my lip nervously.

"Great, welcome to the dream team kid." He said nonchalantly and half sarcastically.

His voice was deep and scratchy; it gave the impression he wanted to kill you. I paused, trying to process his response.

"Wha-what? Just like that? You aren't even afraid of the fact that I have two marks, and you don't even know me!"

His lack of hesitation threw me off. He didn't even know me, and he had just agreed to my help in killing one of the most powerful creatures in the land.

"You wanna help or not, kid? Look, you seem alright; you look like a decent fighter, and about the marks... as long as you don't try to sabotage the mission, why does it matter?"

I thought about the question and let go of my reluctance to trust his trust. I was going to help defeat Cromic, and that was all that mattered - I wasn't about to argue.

"Do you have a plan?" I asked.

"I have the gem. Tomorrow, I'm going to try and put him back into his eternal slumber. We can figure out how you can help in the morning, for now, I want some rest."

"Okay. My friend Falen, he's a siren," I glanced back, motioning at Falen, "Can he help too?"

"Sure, seems like a solid guy, but what's with the dog?"

"His name is Badger; he has healing abilities." Azar looked suspiciously at my dog and narrowed his eyes.

"So," I continued, "He can help me and... uh, you are Tamara, right?" I asked the elf standing by Azar's side.

"Hello! Yes, I'm Tamara!" She said, smiling. Tamara, almost as tall as Azar, was slight in size but appeared strong. I could tell she was prepared, instantly recognizing her lava-proof books and the fashionable yet efficient outfit she wore. She had a bow and sheath of arrows slung on her back and carried a small bag she held in her hand.

"We were just heading to the local tavern. Do you guys need a place to stay?" She asked.

"Yes, actually we do," Falen replied, "When are you going to ambush Cromic though?"

"Tomorrow around midday, but for now, why don't you guys come to the tavern, you both look exhausted," She said empathetically.

We agreed and tiredly followed them to the tavern. Just before we entered, I saw Azar lean in to whisper something to Tamara. I listened intently, trying to hear what he had to say.

"The fates are strong with that dog, I would be cautious if I were you," warned Azar.

Tamara glanced back at the dog and saw me watching them. She nervously smiled and waved before quickly continuing inside. The fates are strong with that dog; I wondered what that meant. I glanced nervously down at my shoes. Do they actually trust me?

Once inside the room Falen and I were sharing I instantly collapsed in the bed, Badger curling up at my side. My dreams were filled with Cromic's gore and destruction. One after another, they rolled in, overwhelming my imagination. At one point, I fell off the side of the mountain as I fought Cromic, and then suddenly, everything shifted, and I was face to face with Cromic. He looked at me, studying my face. Then, as if about to say something, he opened his mouth and spoke. Dragons cannot speak, but Cromic spoke.

"You are an interesting one," he declared calmly.
I opened my mouth to talk to him, but nothing came out.
"Shh," he hushed me, "You can't talk now, you are in a dream."
His voice was oddly similar to Azars, ruff and deep but calm. I didn't understand why Cromic wasn't trying to kill me. His Malus mark seemed to gleam under his right eye.
"Abandon this mission; it's not your destiny to defeat me. You can do so much, but you cannot do this," He said.
My ears burned, and I could feel my face redden, "It's my destiny, no one will stop me!" I wanted to scream at him, but I couldn't.
I tried lunging at him, but I was frozen. He pulled himself out of the volcano and wrapped himself around my motionless body.
"Give up," his words echoed in my head.
I jolted awake, drenched in a cold sweat. The sun was barely on the horizon, a tiny stream of light peeking through the window. With a shaky breath, I stumbled out of bed and threw on an outfit.
What Cromic had said was nothing like the other dreams I had, and it seemed so real.
"You're up early," Falen said as he rubbed his eyes, "Couldn't sleep?" "Yeah," I confessed.
"Same, I had some weird dreams, in one of them, Cromic was a fire-breathing unicorn,"
"You're lucky, all my dreams were about brutally dying," I said, keeping the eerier details to myself.

"Dang, well, let's go see if Azar and Tamara are awake."

We walked over to their room and knocked on their door. Azar answered the door and invited us in.

"Alright, I don't want to take forever on this, but here is the run-down. I already talked to the town mayor and got the gem," Azar placed a green jewel in the middle of our circle, "I'm going to do a spell to put Cromic back into his slumber. Blaire will be guarding me as you two," he said, gesturing at Tamara and Falen, "Will distract Cromic. Blaire, as a fyrian, you can control small amounts of fire or lava, correct?"

"Yes, ever since Cromic re-awakened, I have been practicing more and more, but..." I continued, "Doesn't that make me better on offense?"

"How so? Being able to control the lava won't hurt Cromic, seeing he is immune to it. Instead, you can use it to protect us from Cromics attacks."

My heart sank; I was planning this whole time to attack, but Azar had a point.

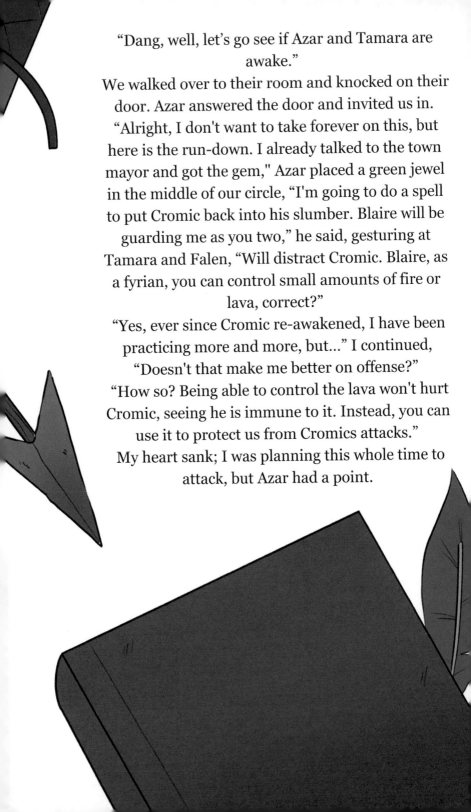

"Alright," I sighed, "How long does it take for the spell to work?"

"I'm not sure, I've never tried it," he explained.

"You couldn't have practiced it before you came?" I asked.

"No, this spell is specifically for dragons. I can't practice it unless I'm practicing on a dragon," Azar explained.

"I'm assuming you don't have any dragon pets," I sighed.

"Nope, but I have been practicing other spells to prepare, don't worry," Azar said.

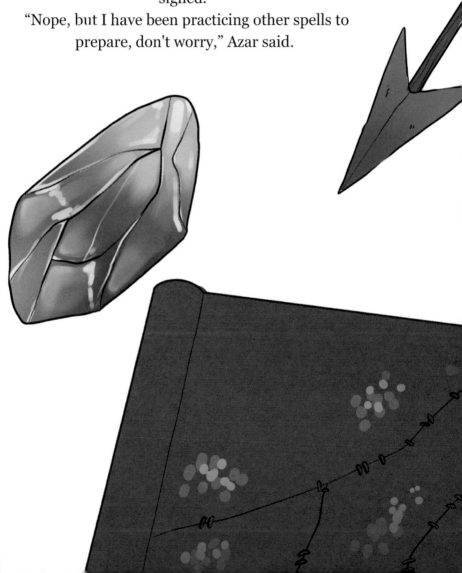

"I have a long-distance bow I can use to shoot from a distance, I saw last night that you have a crossbow; are you trained to use it?" Tamara asked Falen.

Falen grinned and nodded, "Oh yes, I am quite good with it, but if the time comes when I need to attack up close, I also have a dagger," Falen said.

"Good, while Azar is doing his spell, we must distract Cromic in any way we can. We also need to make sure his attention is constantly shifting so he doesn't have time to focus on attacking just one of us. Cromic's talons and teeth are extremely sharp, so try and steer clear of those. He can shoot lava, breathe fire, and fly, though I doubt he will try to fly; he's still adjusting from the eternal slumber and draws strength from being in the lava," explained Tamara.

"Alright, sounds good, anything else we need to cover?" Asked Falen.

"I don't think so, we should go get some breakfast and prepare for battle," said Azar.

We all nodded and made our way to a cafe to get some quick breakfast. We walked in; the cool air was refreshing compared to the scorching heat outside. We sat down at a small booth and read the menus in silence. It was clear we were all nervous. I scanned the page, but I couldn't focus. Eggs, bacon, toast, pancakes... the words swirled in my mind as I desperately tried not to think about the upcoming battle.

The waitress brought water, and I instantly gulped mine down. Sighing, I wiped my sweaty hands on my legs, took a deep breath, and picked the menu back up. A raucous sound shook the ground, piercing the calm, quiet atmosphere of the cafe.

Azar stood up suddenly.

"Come on, we have to go!" he said frantically.

I stood up and hurried outside, heart pounding in my chest.

"What's going on?" Falen asked.

"It's the dragon! We have to go!" yelled Azar.

The giant head of a dragon rose from the top of the mountain; lava spilled over the edges of the mountain, intensifying the heat in the air. We sprinted towards the volcano where Cromic was emerging from the lava.

"Quick, hand me the gem!" Azar hollered at Tamara.

She reached into her bag, pulled out the vibrant green crystal, and handed it to Azar. We stopped at the bottom of the volcano, where the lava was slowly dripping down the sides.

"Is this close enough?" Asked Tamara.

"It should be! Go! Distract Cromic so I can cast the spell!" barked Azar.

Falen and Tamara looked at each other, nodded, and sprinted in opposite directions. My heart was beating furiously as I panted from the long run.

"Alright, do your thing I've got your back!"
I tried to sound confident as I yelled those words at Azar, but the truth is I was freaking out. Eyes closed, I took some deep breaths to steady my breathing. I had been waiting for this moment my whole life, and I couldn't afford to mess up. I opened my eyes and stared bitterly at the lava dragon.

Shouts sounded from either side of the mountain, calling to get Cromic's attention. The murmur of unrecognizable words from behind me told me that Azar had started the spell. Suddenly, the dragon's attention shifted toward Azar. Cromic opened his mouth, his attack impending.

I jerked and threw up my arms, channeling my power to deflect the lava. Silence, then blazing heat as lava spewed from Cromic's mouth and parted in the air around us. Breathing hard, I concentrated on separating the lava. The muttering behind me got louder, and I could see a faint green light out of the corner of my eye. Just as I thought I was about to pass out from exhaustion, the lava suddenly stopped.

The grass around us was coated in a thick layer of boiling lava, and ahead of us, Cromic's attention had shifted to Falen. Cromic opened his mouth and shot lava at Falen, but Falen rolled to the side, narrowly avoiding the attack. Tamara was shooting arrows at lightning speed from behind, trying to catch Cromic's attention, but he was laser-focused on Falen.

A strong feeling that if I didn't help Falen, somehow he would die urged me into motion. I frantically gathered the lava, channeling my power to form it into a huge sphere, and I shot it at Cromic's face. The lava hit him, and he let out an enraged roar as he turned to face me.

Behind me, the light was growing stronger and stronger as Azar continued chanting the spell.

Ahead of me, Tamara shot an arrow piercing Cromic's wing. Cromic roared again and pulled himself further out of the lava, his torso and back legs now visible. He sat on the edge of the volcano, just like on the cover of the book. The sheer size of his body compared to the volcano was huge, it was crazy to think Cromic fit in there.

Turning back toward me, Cromic opened his mouth, this time, to attack with fire. Again, I deflected his attack, tilting the flames above us to the ash-filled sky. I wavered, lightheaded, but held my stance, withdrawing all of my power to protect us.

The flames stopped as quickly as they started as Cromic's attention turned to Tamara, whose arrow had perfectly pierced the center of what had been Cromic's good eye. Blood dripped off the end of the arrow, and Cromic let out a low, vicious growl before unleashing a fire attack at Tamara. It was unlike his other attacks, quicker and less predictable and impossible for Tamara to avoid. The flames roared down on her. How could he survive this? My body went numb, Is she going to die?

Then, coughing and wheezing, Tamara crawled out from the flames. Only my duty to protect Azar stopped me from running to her. She clutched her chest and leaned back into the side of the mountain. Her clothes were seared, and she was emanating smoke, but she was alive - Azar needed to hurry up if he wanted her to continue that way. There was no way she could continue fighting; she would have to lay low until we could help her. I thought of Badger, not regretting my decision to leave him behind at the cafe but still wishing we had his power to heal Tamara now. As if summoned by my thoughts, there he was, standing right next to me. He looked up at me, his big blue eyes staring into mine, and then as if reading my mind, he took off towards the volcano.

In awe, I watched as he ran up to Tamara and then licked her hand. He wagged his tail happily and laid down next to her as he continued to lick her hand and face. The relief I felt was short-lived as I saw Cromic shooting lava at Falen and Falen, barely evading the attacks.

The green light emanating from behind me was almost blinding now, and then, it stopped. Everything went quiet, and for a moment, it felt like time froze. Then, stepping back into the lava, Cromic disappeared.

Falen let out a victorious "Whoop!" Azar cheered along with him.

Cromic was gone. We had won. It all hit me like a boulder: the relief, the realization. I grinned and looked back at Azar, who couldn't contain his smile.

"We just did that," I remarked, still grinning.

Falen sprinted up to us, his smile brighter than Cromic's lava, "Holy fates, that was awesome!" He exclaimed.

I hugged him, and Azar joined in, celebrating our victory. But something was nagging at me, like something important we forgot to do.

"Tamara!" I exclaimed, running over to where she was lying against the volcano.

She smiled at me softly, "Did we win?" she asked
hopefully.
"Yes, we did," I said.
It was surreal; I had to hold back tears of joy.
Badger and the four of us sat in silence, processing
everything that just took place, and then, we
rejoiced until sunset, watching as the sun dipped
down the horizon.
With our help, Tamara got up, and we walked back
to the Tavern, people calling out and cheering for us
on the way.
"I can't believe you saved us! So, what will your
next quest be?" A woman asked.
We all looked at each other and laughed.
"I don't know, but we sure do make a good team,"
Azar remarked.
At that moment, I knew there was a change in the
world and that we were a team destined to do great
things. I had a feeling this wasn't the end of my
journey, that there was much more to come, and I
knew my team knew it too.

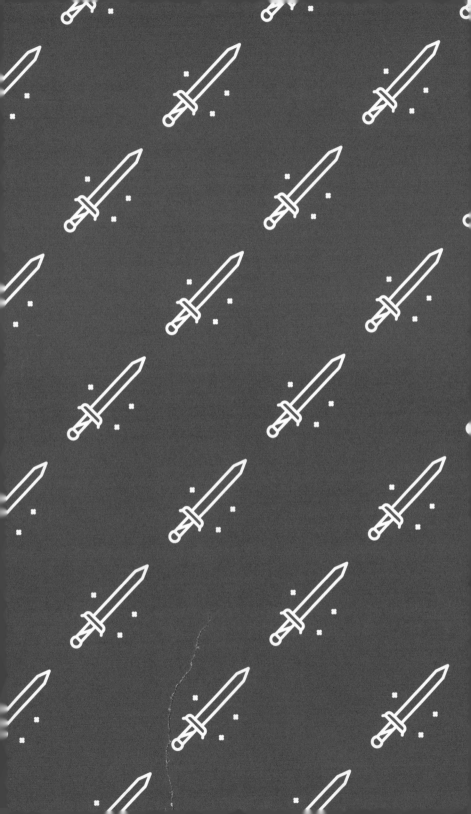

THE END

A PEEK AT THE ORIGINAL BOOK

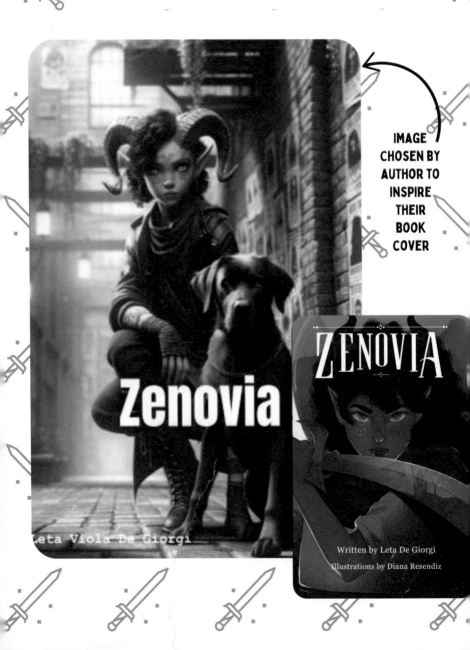

IMAGE CHOSEN BY AUTHOR TO INSPIRE THEIR BOOK COVER

Zenovia

Leta Viola De Giorgi

ZENOVIA

Written by Leta De Giorgi

Illustrations by Diana Resendiz

About the Author

Leta De Giorgi is a creative, bilingual 11-year-old with a passion for writing. She is Italian-born and moved to Colorado, where she was raised. The middle child of three and the only girl, Leta found a love of writing early on and a way to share her stories with the world. Her writing transports the reader to magical worlds full of adventure and possibilities. Leta's passion for storytelling can also be seen in her amazing artwork and her love for music. Named after a famous tiny church in Tuscany, Vita Leta, which means "happy life", brings joy to others through her self-expression, kindness, and thoughtful soul.

About the artist

Diana Resendiz lives in Queretaro, Mexico. She is a 26-year-old wife, mom and digital Artist who likes to bring life to other people's ideas using her skills.

Made in the USA
Columbia, SC
18 November 2024

46754236R00042